the kind little crocodile

by Cleo & Greg Duggan

"teach a child to choose the right path, and when they are older, they will remain upon it."

Proverbs 22:6

Cleo & Greg Duggan

With God's love in our heart, let the story now start.

In the heart of a busy river, where the water flowed quickly and the wildlife thrived, lived a young crocodile named Cody. Unlike the other crocodiles who were fierce and angry, Cody had a gentle and kind heart.

While his sharp teeth made him look fearsome, he believed that you should be kind to your neighbour, as Jesus taught.

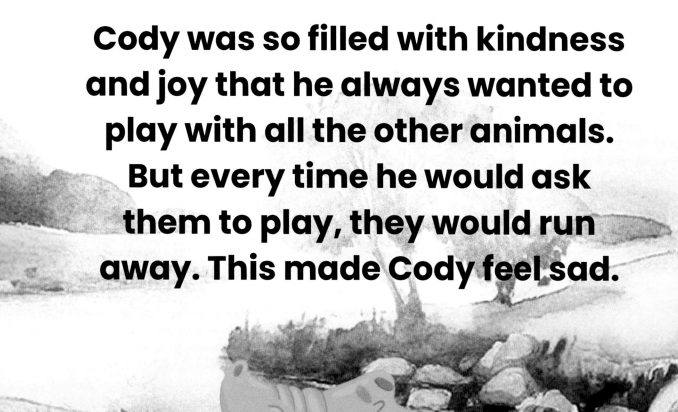

Cody was so filled with kindness and joy that he always wanted to play with all the other animals. But every time he would ask them to play, they would run away. This made Cody feel sad.

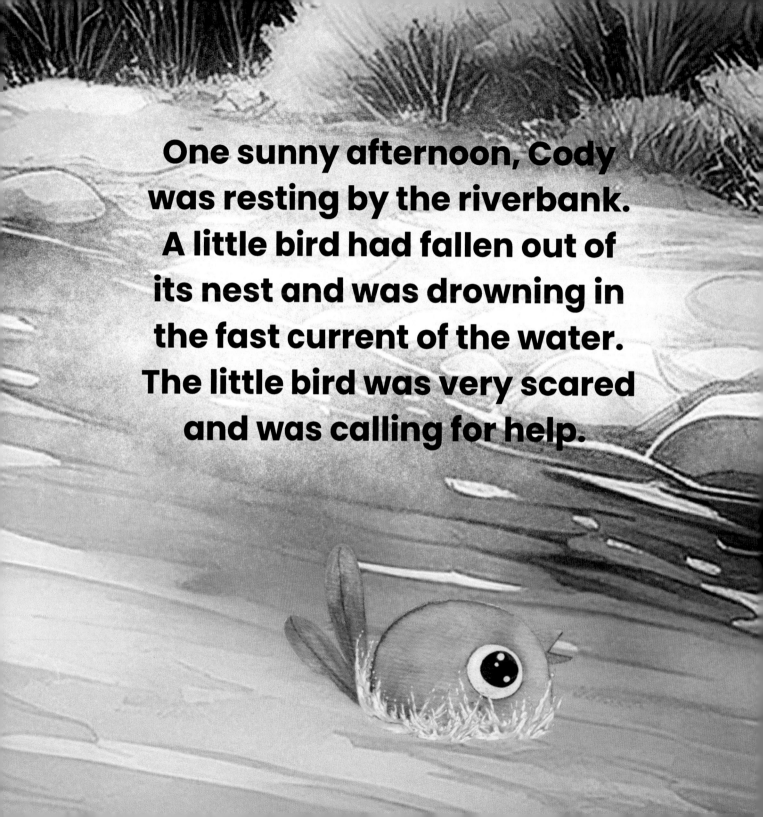

One sunny afternoon, Cody was resting by the riverbank. A little bird had fallen out of its nest and was drowning in the fast current of the water. The little bird was very scared and was calling for help.

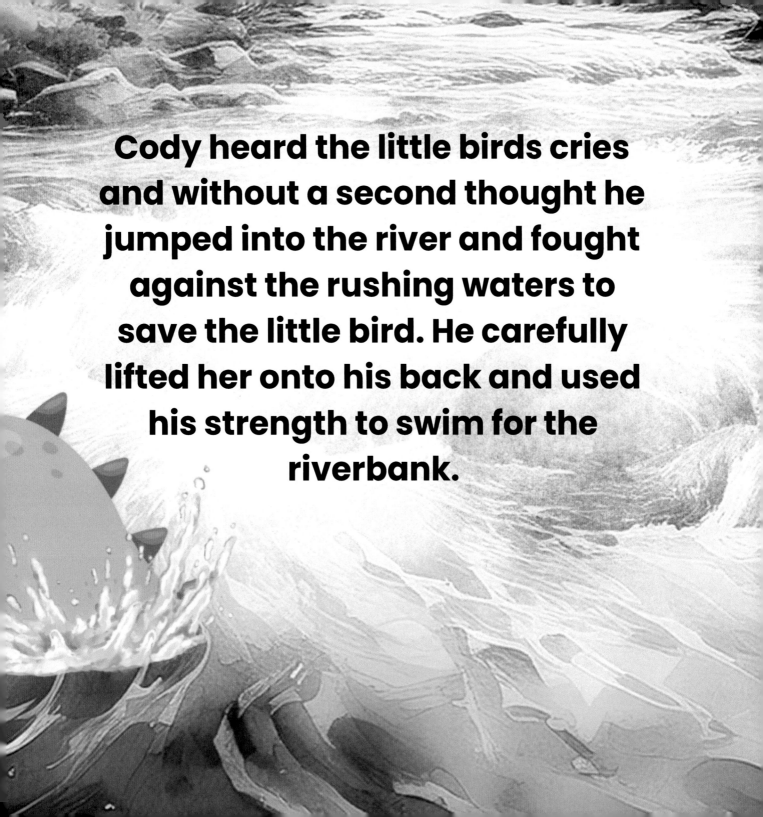

Cody heard the little birds cries and without a second thought he jumped into the river and fought against the rushing waters to save the little bird. He carefully lifted her onto his back and used his strength to swim for the riverbank.

Cody gently placed the little bird on the shore.

The little bird's whole family came to the river bank and celebrated, saying thank you to Cody for saving their baby. "That's okay," said Cody, "I just wanted to be kind, as Jesus is always kind to me."

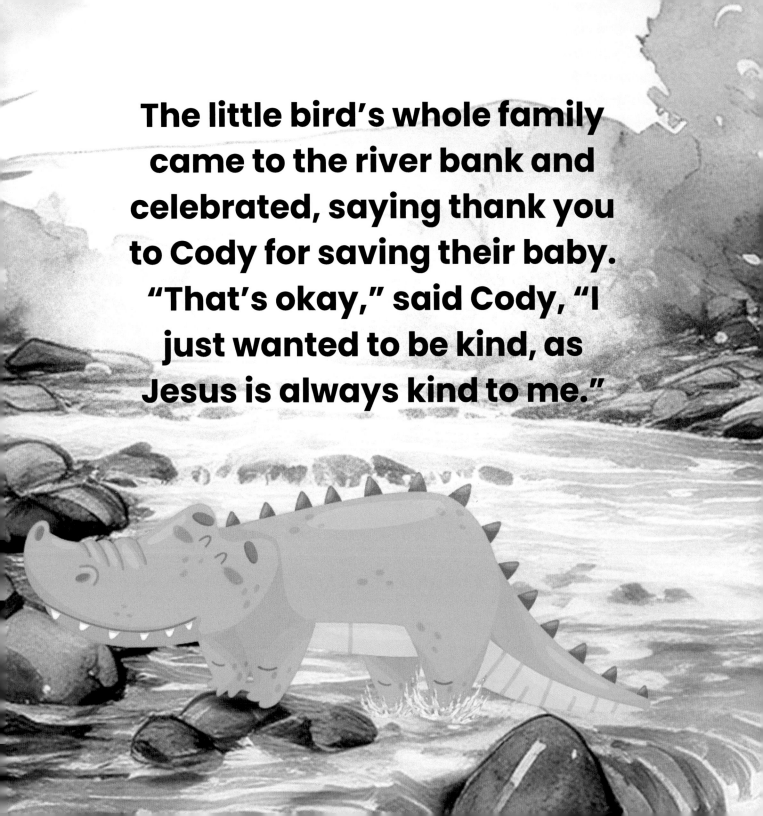

The story of what Cody had done spread around the river, and the animals all thought he had been very brave and kind.

But still, when Cody would ask the animals to play with him, they would run away scared saying "We don't want to play with you, go away!"

Later that Autumn, dark clouds gathered over the river, and a big storm completely flooded the riverbank. The water levels rose so quickly that the animals had to climb up in to the trees. They were trapped and shouting for help, but they didn't know who could save them.

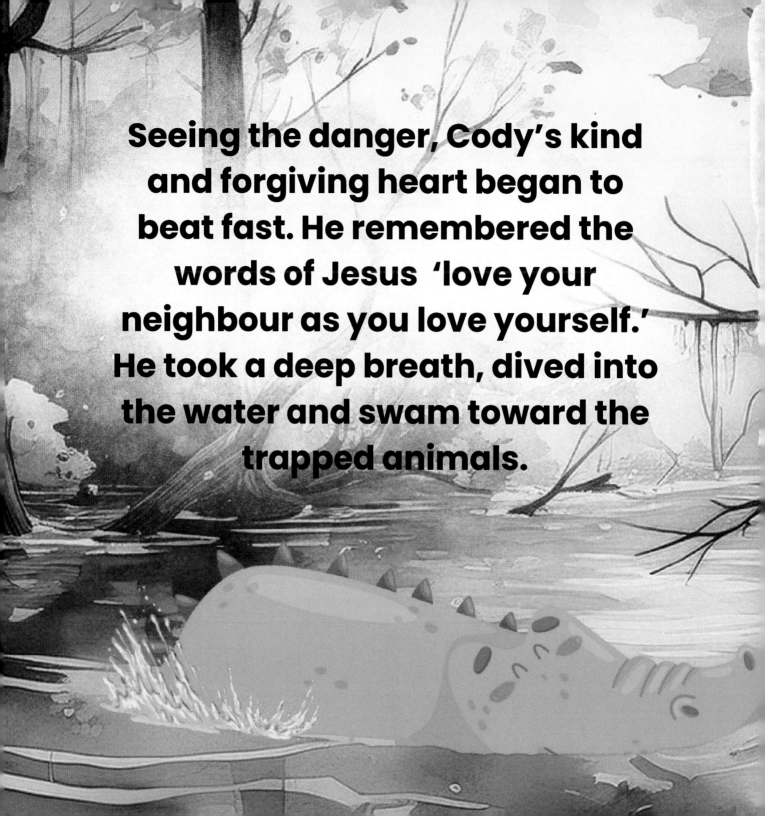

Seeing the danger, Cody's kind and forgiving heart began to beat fast. He remembered the words of Jesus 'love your neighbour as you love yourself.' He took a deep breath, dived into the water and swam toward the trapped animals.

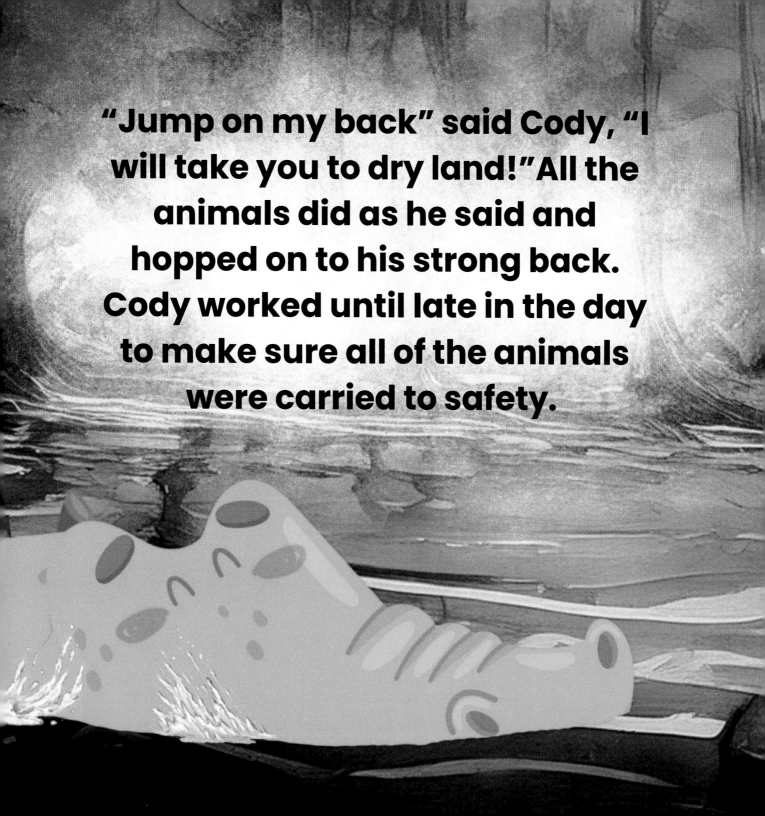

"Jump on my back" said Cody, "I will take you to dry land!"All the animals did as he said and hopped on to his strong back. Cody worked until late in the day to make sure all of the animals were carried to safety.

Once all the animals were safely on the beach, they clapped for joy and thanked Cody for his kindness.

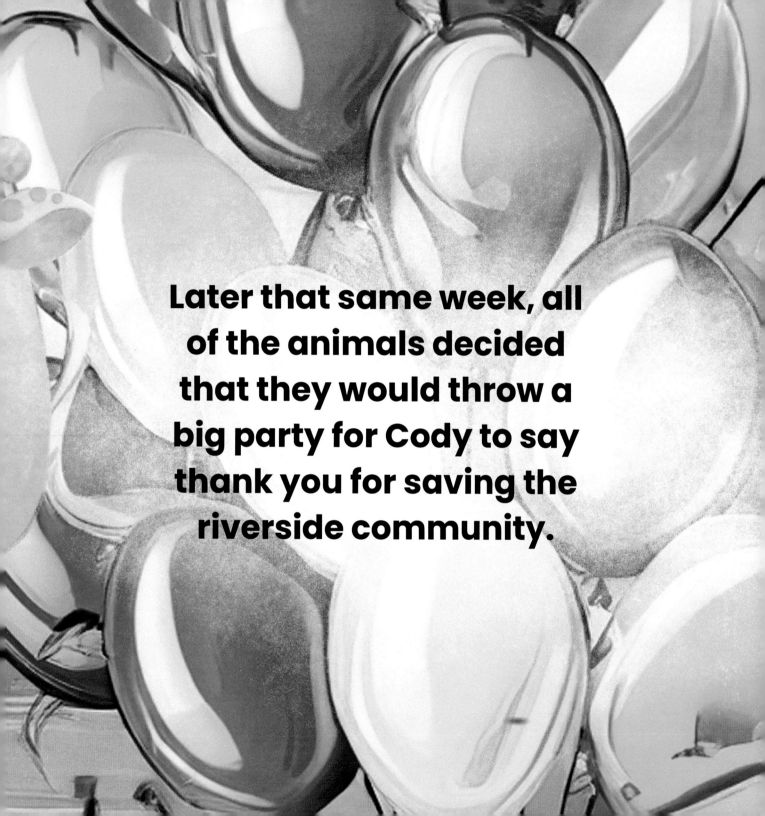

Later that same week, all of the animals decided that they would throw a big party for Cody to say thank you for saving the riverside community.

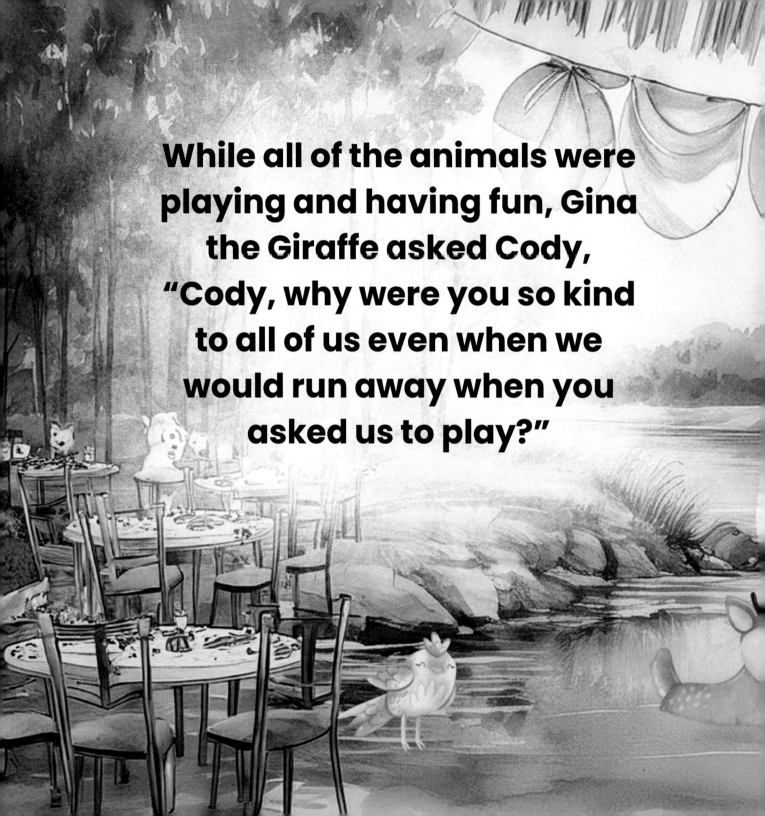

While all of the animals were playing and having fun, Gina the Giraffe asked Cody, "Cody, why were you so kind to all of us even when we would run away when you asked us to play?"

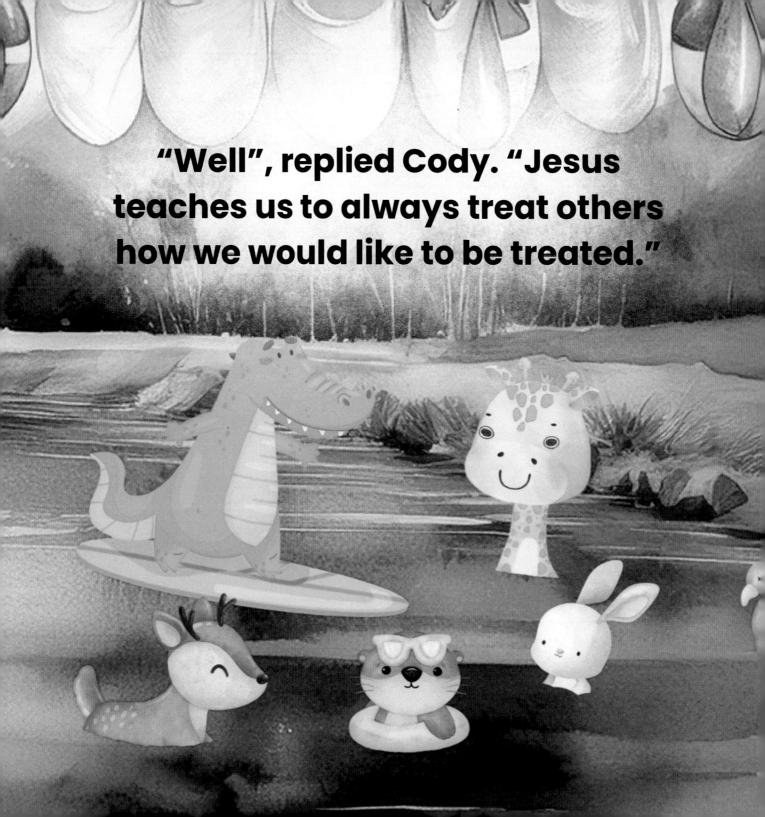

"Well", replied Cody. "Jesus teaches us to always treat others how we would like to be treated."

Gina replied, "So you were kind to us because you hoped one day that we would be kind to you?" "Yes exactly", said Cody, "and because I followed the words of Jesus, we are all friends now having a big party!"

Gina replied "Wow, can we all follow Jesus too?"
Cody replied "Of course, Jesus will always welcome you with loving arms!"

From that day on, all of the animals, including the other crocodiles, began to be more kind and loving to one another.

They would all meet at their little river church and read their Bibles together, always thanking God for the beautiful teachings of Jesus.

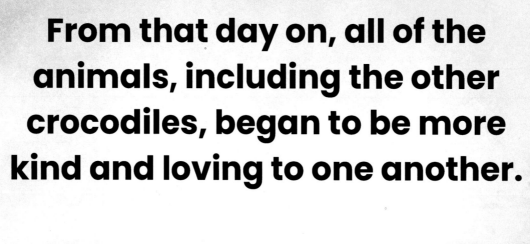

CUT OUT & LAMINATE YOUR SELF CONTROL KEYCHAIN!

Collect All the Keychains In Our Other Books!

God's Light Guides My Way.

God's Joy Fills My Soul.

In God's Hands, I'm Safe.

With God, I Am Brave.

God's Hope Lifts My Spirit.

God's Mercy Comforts Me.

SOME QUESTIONS ABOUT THE STORY!

- How did Cody show kindness to the other animals?

- Why did Cody decide to show kindness to the other animals, even when they wouldn't play with him?

- Can you remember the last time someone was kind to you? How did it make you feel?

Made in the USA
Las Vegas, NV
02 January 2025

15739827R00021